D1604763

THE MARK OF ZORRO®

ORIGINAL BY JOHNSTON McCULLEY

RETOLD BY PAULINE FRANCIS

Published in the United States by Windmill Books
(Skyview Books)

Windmill Books
303 Park Avenue South
Suite #1280
New York, NY 10010-3657

U.S. publication copyright © Evans Brothers Limited 2009
First North American Edition

© 2009 Zorro Productions, Inc. All rights reserved

Library of Congress Cataloging-in-Publication Data
Francis, Pauline
    The mark of Zorro / original by Johnston McCulley ; retold by Pauline Franci
cm. – (Foundation classics)
        Includes index.
        Summary: Zorro makes it his mission to save the people of California from a
abusive and corrupt governor and his army.
        ISBN 978-1-60754-011-3
        1. Zorro (Fictitious character)—Juvenile fiction   2. Aristocracy (Social clas
Juvenile fiction   3. Vigilantes—Juvenile fiction   [1. Aristocracy (Social class)—Fic
2. Vigilantes—Fiction]   I. McCulley, Johnston, 1883-1958
II. Title   III. Series
        [Fic]—dc22

13-digit ISBN: 978-1-60754-011-3
Manufactured in China

THE MARK OF ZORRO

Introduction

Johnston McCulley was born in 1879 in Ottawa, Illinois. He worked as crime reporter for a newspaper, but often wrote cowboy stories for weekly magazines. In 1919, McCulley created a new character called Zorro for five of his stories. They were made into a film in 1920. The stories were so popular that they were published as a book in 1924 – using the film's title *"The Mark of Zorro."*

The Zorro stories are set in the small town of Reina de Los Angeles (Queen of the Angels), in southern California. This town is now the city of Los Angeles. California was then a province of Mexico and its people spoke Spanish. Many Franciscan monks went there to set up missions. They owned much of the land and raised cattle to sell cattle hides.

Zorro was a man who appeared in times of trouble wearing a long purple cloak and a black mask. He fought with a sword in one hand and a pistol in the other. He helped the poor and always stood up for what was right. In *The Mark of Zorro*, he helps a friar and a noble family whose land has been stolen – and falls in love!

More than eighty films based on Zorro have been made throughout the world. He was such a well-loved character that Johnston McCulley wrote stories about him until his death in 1958, at the age of seventy-nine.

CHAPTER ONE

The Stranger in the Storm

It was a typical February storm for southern California. The wind shrieked and sheets of rain hit the ground in the little town of Reina de Los Angeles. But inside the tavern, Sergeant Pedro Gonzales stretched his big feet toward the roaring fire. With one hand he touched his sword and in the other he held a mug of wine.

"'Tis a night for evil!" he said to the landlord.

The landlord agreed and filled the sergeant's mug again. Pedro Gonzales had a bad temper when it was empty.

"An evil night!" the sergeant repeated. He drank his wine in one gulp and sprawled closer to the fire.

The conversation died away and the landlord became afraid. Sergeant Gonzales was only happy when he was arguing and if he could not argue, he might start a fight. The landlord came closer and started to speak. "They are saying in the town that this Senor Zorro is causing trouble again."

His words had a terrible effect on Gonzales. He hurled his half-filled wine mug onto the dirt floor and crashed his fist onto the table. The other soldiers scattered.

"Senor Zorro, eh?" he cried in a ferocious voice. "Is it my fate to always hear that name? Senor Zorro, eh? Mr. Fox! He is as cunning as one, and he stinks as much!"

Gonzales turned to face his soldiers. "He is the curse of the highway with his mask and sword, they tell me. He uses the point of it to carve the letter 'Z' on the face of his enemy. The mark of Zorro, that's what they call it. But I have never seen him or his sword. No, Senor Zorro never comes near me. Here is one fox it will give me pleasure to hunt."

"There is a reward…" the landlord began.

"Yes," Gonzales interrupted, "offered by the Governor of California himself. But Senor Zorro never visits our town. Why not? Because we have a prison, that's why! And Senor Zorro keeps away from prisons."

"But he must have a place where he eats and sleeps," the landlord said. "One day your soldiers will trail him to his den."

"He says that he is not a thief," Gonzales sneered. "He says that he is a friend of the poor and that he only punishes those who behave badly."

"I am glad that he never comes here," the landlord said. "I have no wish to be robbed."

"To be robbed?" Gonzales cried in a voice of thunder. "Robbed of what? Of a jug of weak wine. You fool! Let this bold and cunning Zorro enter this door. Let his eyes twinkle through his mask. Let me face him just for one moment and I shall claim that generous reward. More wine, fat fool!"

The door of the tavern suddenly opened and the candles

flickered in a gust of wind and rain. Gonzales half pulled out his sword. The landlord gave a sigh of relief. It was Don Diego Vega, a fair young nobleman of twenty-four.

"Have I startled you, senores?" Don Diego asked politely, glancing around the room.

"No, the storm did," Gonzales replied. "You are not capable of startling any man."

"Hmm!" Don Diego grunted, taking off his hat and cloak. "Watch your words, my friend. I can forget the difference in our upbringing only if you mind your tongue. You amuse me, senor, and for that I do not mind buying you wine. But make fun of me in public, or in private, and we shall no longer be friends."

"I beg your pardon, my good friend," Gonzales replied. "If any man asks me from now on, I shall tell them that you are a man of quick wit and sword." He threw back his head and roared with laughter.

The peculiar friendship between the two men was the talk of the town. Don Diego came from a family that owned thousand of acres of land, herds of horses and cattle – and huge fields of wheat. He owned an enormous ranch and a house in the town, too. One day, he would inherit a great fortune.

But Don Diego was unlike most other young men. He hardly ever wore a sword. He disliked fighting. He was the opposite of Sergeant Gonzales in every way.

"We have been talking about Senor Zorro," Gonzales said. "The curse of the highway."

"Let us not speak about him," Don Diego said with a yawn. "All I ever hear are tales of bloodshed and violence. These are difficult times. Is it not possible to talk of music or poetry?"

"Corn mush and goat's milk," Gonzales muttered.

"In any case, Senor Zorro has only robbed men who have stolen from the missions or the poor," Don Diego continued. "He has killed no one."

"I shall catch him!" Gonzales cried. "And…"

"Then tell me later – not now!" Don Diego replied. He put down his wine and reached for his sombrero and cloak. Then he plunged back into the storm and the darkness.

"That man is as gentle as a spring breeze," Gonzales remarked. "He cannot bear violence. I wish I had his looks and money. Ha! There would be a stream of broken hearts."

"And broken heads!" one of the soldiers said.

"Ha! Ha! Yes, broken heads!" cried Gonzales, jumping to his feet. He pulled out his sword and swept it backward and forward through the air, shouting, thrusting and lunging. He roared with laughter as he fought the shadows.

"If only this fine Senor Zorro was here!" Gonzales gasped.

The door opened again and a man entered. His sombrero was pulled low on his head to stop the wind carrying it away. His body was wrapped in a long purple cloak.

Suddenly the stranger whirled round. The landlord gave a cry of fear and moved away. The soldiers gasped. Sergeant Gonzales allowed his lower jaw to drop and his eyes bulged. The man who stood before them wore a black mask over his face. His eyes glittered behind two slits. He bowed.

"Senor Zorro, at your service," he said.

CHAPTER TWO

A Clash of Swords

"By all the saints, if you are Senor Zorro, then you are a fool!" Gonzales cried. "By coming here, you have walked into a trap, my fine highwayman. Have you come to surrender your sword to me?"

Zorro laughed. "No. I am here on business." He stared at Gonzales. "Four days ago, you beat a man brutally on the road between here and the mission at San Gabriel."

"What business is that of yours?"

"I have come to punish you," Zorro said.

"Come to punish me?" Gonzales asked, laughing. "You are as good as dead, senor. Say your prayers now!"

"There is no need," Zorro replied.

"Then I must do my duty," Gonzales replied. He lifted the point of his sword and walked carefully toward Zorro. Then suddenly, he stepped back. Zorro was holding a pistol in front of him.

"Ha! So that is the way you do it!" Gonzales cried. "Gentlemen prefer the sword."

"Move back!" Zorro cried. "I shall not warn you again. I shall use my sword when everybody else in this room has moved away from me. I shall hold my pistol in my left hand

and fight the sergeant with the sword in my right hand." He laughed loudly. "On guard, senor!"

Gonzales raised his sword and their blades clashed. Zorro did not move. He did not step forward or to the side. Gonzales attacked furiously. Then he moved away, hoping that Zorro would follow. But he stood his ground, forcing Gonzales to attack again.

Anger got the better of the sergeant. "Don't stand there like a mountain!" he cried. Then he tried to control his anger for an angry man cannot control his sword. His eyes narrowed and his stare became cold. But all the tricks he tried had no effect. Through his mask, Zorro's eyes seemed to be laughing at him.

"We have had enough of playing," Zorro said. "It is time for the punishment."

Suddenly he began to walk forward, slowly forcing Gonzales back until he was against the wall. At the same moment, somebody banged on the bolted door.

"I regret that I do not have time to give you the punishment you deserve," Zorro cried.

"We have Senor Zorro in here!" Gonzales cried. Zorro's sword darted backward and forward, glittering in the candlelight, until Gonzales felt his sword torn from his hand. He waited for the final thrust of the blade.

"I shall die here instead of on the field of battle as a soldier should," he thought.

Instead, Zorro slapped Pedro Gonzales once across the cheek. "Until next time, senor!" he said.

He ran to the window, opened it and jumped out. The wind and rain rushed in, blowing out all the candles. Gonzales roared with shame. He and his men stumbled after Zorro. But it was no use. It was too dark and wet to see anything.

Senor Zorro had disappeared – and no man could tell where.

CHAPTER THREE

A Proposal of Marriage

The sky was a perfect blue the next morning and the sun shone brightly. Don Diego came from his house and climbed carefully onto his waiting horse. The men in the plaza grinned as they watched him. Young men these days usually jumped onto their horses and disappeared in a cloud of dust.

But Don Diego walked his horse slowly to the edge of the town. Then he cantered into the countryside. After four miles, he turned from the highway into a narrow, dusty trail that led to a hacienda. He was going to visit Don Carlos Pulido.

Don Carlos used to be as wealthy as Don Diego. But now he had only a small part of his fortune – and his noble name. The Governor of California had taken away most of his land because he did not like him. Don Carlos had a wife and one child, the senorita Lolita, who was eighteen years old.

When he saw the rider approaching, Don Carlos ordered his servant to bring out small cakes and wine. Then he walked down the steps and held out his hand to Don Diego.

"It is a long and dusty road," Don Diego said. "Such a journey has tired me."

Don Carlos stopped himself from smiling as he

remembered what a weak man his visitor was.

"I am glad to see you have come to visit my poor hacienda," he said. "How are things in Reina de Los Angeles?"

"Everything is the same," Don Diego replied, "except that this Senor Zorro invaded the tavern last night. He had a duel with the big Sergeant Gonzales. Then he escaped through a window."

"A clever rogue!" Don Carlos exclaimed. "At least I have nothing to fear from him. I have little left except my hacienda."

"That is a pity!" Don Diego said. He sipped his wine. "My father has been urging me to marry, senor. A man of my position and fortune should have a wife and children. So I have come to speak to you about it, Senor Carlos."

"To me?" his friend gasped.

"I must marry a woman of good blood. You may have fallen on hard times … but, senor, your family has the most noble blood in the land. And an only daughter, Senorita Lolita. That is why I am here today."

Don Carlos was delighted. A marriage between a Vega and his daughter! He would be powerful again.

"Just let me know when the wedding can take place," Don Diego said.

Don Carlos was annoyed. "Would you like to see my daughter now?" he asked.

15

"If I must," Don Diego replied.

Lolita was a dainty girl with black eyes and black hair coiled around her head. Her tiny feet peeped out from below a brightly colored skirt.

"You are as beautiful as you were when I last saw you," Don Diego said.

"Always tell a senorita that she is more beautiful," Don Carlos groaned, leaving them alone together.

"Will you agree to be my wife?" Don Diego asked in a timid voice. "It will save me the trouble of riding out here again."

Senorita Lolita's face flushed. "The man who marries me must win my love," she cried. "And he must be a man with energy." She walked back angrily to the house.

Don Carlos watched Don Diego ride off. "You cannot throw away such a fine chance, Lolita," he said with a sigh.

At siesta time, when everybody else was sleeping, Senorita Lolita went to sit on a bench by the fountain. "I do not know what to do," she thought. "I do not want to marry a weak man like Don Diego, but I should like to see my father rich and important again."

Soon the sound of the water lulled Lolita to sleep, too, until a touch on the arm woke her up. In front of her stood a man wearing a long cloak, his face covered with a black mask.

"Are you…?" she began, terrified.

"Yes, I am Senor Zorro," he replied, bowing low. "I mean you no harm. I punish only those people who are unjust and your father is not that. I am tired and I thought this would be a good place to rest for a while. But I saw you out here and I had to come closer to admire your beauty. Then I had to speak to you."

"I wish my beauty affected other men in this way," Lolita said, blushing.

Zorro sat down on the bench, raised the bottom of his mask and kissed her hand.

"You must go, senor!" she cried. "There is a large reward for your capture."

He kissed her hand once more before he left. And the senorita Lolita watched him ride away, her heart pounding.

"If only Don Diego had such life and courage," she whispered to herself.

CHAPTER FOUR

Zorro Rides Again

That same evening, just as Don Carlos was about to eat with his wife and daughter, somebody knocked at the door.

It was Senor Zorro.

Senorita Lolita gasped at his courage. But her father shouted at him. "Scoundrel!" he bellowed. "How dare you enter an honest house? What do you want?"

"I wish for food and drink, that is all," Zorro replied. "If the Governor hears about this, you can tell everybody that I forced you." As he spoke, Zorro took out his pistol. Don Carlos' wife shrieked and fainted.

"Take your wife to her bedroom," Zorro said kindly. "Your daughter will remain here as my hostage." As soon as they were alone, Zorro went over to the senorita Lolita. "I had to see you again," he whispered.

"You must never come here again!" she whispered back.

When Don Carlos returned, he and his daughter were forced to sit at the other side of the room so that Zorro could raise the bottom of his mask to eat. But he soon guessed that Don Carlos had sent for help while he was out of the room. Zorro was not mistaken. As he was preparing to leave, a terrified servant appeared. "There are soldiers surrounding the house!" he shouted.

Zorro jumped onto the table and knocked the candlestick to the floor, plunging the room into darkness. Don Carlos bellowed like a bull to bring in Sergeant Gonzales and his soldiers. Then Zorro rushed through the kitchen to the patio. A high-pitched sound filled the air, followed by the noise of a galloping horse.

"He has escaped!" Gonzales shrieked. "After him!"

When the soldiers had ridden off into the darkness, Don Carlos heard the sound of a horse approaching. He ordered his servant to bring his sword. But it was not the highwayman returning. It was Captain Ramon who was in charge of the town's army barracks.

"I am looking for my men," he explained. Then he caught sight of Senorita Lolita. "But I can wait here for them to return." He sighed. "I should make short work of Zorro if I met him. He has killed men and insulted women. He…"

A nearby door flew open – and Zorro stepped into the room. "You lie!" he said.

"There shall be no escape for you now," Captain Ramon shouted, pulling out his sword.

"I thought you had escaped," Don Carlos wailed.

"Ha! A trick!" Zorro replied, laughing. "Did you hear that strange cry just now? My horse is trained to gallop off when he hears it. The soldiers follow. Then he hides and waits for me."

Zorro took out his sword and the two men fought

furiously. Captain Ramon gave Zorro no rest and kept him close to the wall. But at last Zorro forced him back into a corner. Then he stabbed Captain Ramon in the left shoulder.

He turned and bowed to the senorita Lolita. "I am sorry that you have had to see this," he said. "The captain is not badly injured. And this time, I really am leaving."

Zorro laughed, put on his sombrero and ran out to his waiting horse.

A few minutes later, Don Diego rode slowly up to the hacienda. "Ha! I am pleased to find you all safe and well," he said. "I heard that Senor Zorro was in the neighborhood. But I find my journey has been for nothing. A mug of your wine, Don Carlos. I am tired." He collapsed into a chair.

"It is not much of a journey – four miles," Captain Ramon said.

"Not for a soldier," Don Diego replied, "but it is a long way for a gentleman."

"Can a soldier not be a gentleman?" Captain Ramon asked angrily. "By all the saints! Are you saying that I am not of good blood?"

"I do not know since I have not seen your blood," Don Diego replied, glancing at the captain's shoulder. "No doubt Senor Zorro could answer that question." He went to sit beside Senorita Lolita. "Have you thought about what I said this morning?" he asked quietly. "I should like to marry you as soon as possible."

Lolita bit her lip with anger. And on the other side of the room, Captain Ramon was asking Don Carlos for permission to court her!

"Don Diego asked me the same question this morning," Don Carlos replied. "If he fails to touch her heart, then … yes, you may."

"Then it is between Don Diego and myself," the captain replied.

That night, Senorita Lolita could not sleep. She sat looking through her window, her mind full of thoughts of Senor Zorro.

"I wish he were not a highwayman," she sighed. "How I could love such a man!"

CHAPTER FIVE

Love at Last

The following morning, just after dawn, the plaza was full of soldiers. They were preparing to hunt down Zorro.

"I do not intend to come back until I have captured him or until I die trying to capture him," Sergeant Gonzales said to himself.

Don Diego, disturbed by the noise, opened his front door. "You are making enough noise to wake the dead," he complained. "Which way are you going after Senor Zorro?"

"Toward the town of Pala," Gonzales replied.

Gonzales and his men mounted their horses and rode off. When they were a tiny cloud of dust, Don Diego ordered his servant to bring out his horse. As he waited, he wrote this letter:

> *Don Carlos*
> *While the soldiers are hunting down Senor Zorro,*
> *I beg you to come and stay in my town house. You*
> *will be safer there. I shall be away for two or three*
> *days.*
> *Don Diego.*

Don Carlos was pleased to receive this letter. He and his wife wanted to be seen to be the guests of such an important man as Don Diego Vega. So they rode immediately to Reina de Los Angeles.

Captain Ramon lost no time in coming to pay a visit. He wanted to see Senorita Lolita again. Unfortunately, her parents were out.

"It is not proper for you to be here alone with me," she begged, a little frightened. "You must leave now."

"Your father should be proud that I am interested in you," he said, taking her hand. "Will you do me the honor of becoming my wife? If you marry me, I shall ask the Governor to give your father back some of his land."

Senorita Lolita pulled away from him, angry. "I shall only marry a gentleman!" she cried, "and you are certainly not that!"

"But you would sell yourself to Diego to solve your father's problems!" he said.

Like a flash of lightning, Lolita sprang forward and slapped Ramon's cheek. But he caught hold of her arm and held her tightly so that she could not hit him again.

"One moment, senor!" a deep voice said.

Ramon let go and swore loudly. There, right in front of him, stood Senor Zorro.

"You deserve to die, captain," Zorro said, "but I shall not kill you. You will go down on your knees and apologize to the senorita. Then you will leave this house. On your knees, senor! Say it, or I shall kill you."

Captain Ramon did as he ordered. Then Zorro lifted him from his feet and hurled him into the darkness.

"Thank you," Lolita cried. "Thank you! Now go before my parents return. Become an honest man and I will marry you."

"I still have work to do, senorita," Zorro replied. "But when it is finished, I shall come back to you."

"Please, senor," she sobbed. "I love you."

Senor Zorro wrapped his cloak around him. Then he ran to the window and the darkness outside swallowed him up.

CHAPTER SIX

The Letter

Captain Ramon picked himself up from the dusty ground and ran back to the army barracks. His face was purple with anger. There were not enough men left to send after Zorro. Most of them were already chasing him.

"I cannot let it be known that Senor Zorro has insulted me," he thought, "but there must be another way of avenging myself on Don Carlos."

He paced up and down. At last, he sat down at his desk to write a letter to his friend, the Governor of California, who lived in San Francisco de Asis in northern California.

"...I regret to inform you that Senor Zorro has not yet been captured, but he is being pursued as I write. I have to tell you that Zorro does not fight alone. He has been sheltered and fed by Don Carlos Pulido, a gentleman who already dislikes you..."

Captain Ramon grinned as he finished his letter and wrote a copy of it. Then he gave it to one of his soldiers to ride to the Governor as fast as he could. As he sat reading the copy, he did not know that Zorro was watching him through the window. He heard Captain Ramon talking to himself. "That will teach the pretty senorita a lesson," he was muttering.

Zorro's face grew black with rage. He wrapped his cloak around him and made his way to Captain Ramon's office. He did not knock. He walked toward him slowly, holding his pistol in front of him.

"Not a sound, senor," he warned the captain, "or you die."

"What are you doing here?" Captain Ramon whispered.

"I want to read your letter," Zorro replied, picking up the copy. He read it quickly. Then he held it to the flame of a candle. "So you fight women now, senor?" he asked. "I regret that you are not well enough to duel with me."

Suddenly, they heard the sound of horses and Gonzales' loud voice.

"Gonzales!" Captain Ramon shrieked. "Zorro is here!"

As Gonzales rushed into the room, Zorro drew his sword and knocked the candles from the table. Then he moved silently along the wall until he came to the captain's chair.

"Catch him!" Captain Ramon cried. "How can one man make fools of the lot of…?" He stopped speaking as Zorro grasped him from behind.

"Soldiers, I have your captain!" Zorro shouted. "I am going to the outside door. If anybody attacks, I'll shoot him."

Holding Captain Ramon in front of him, Zorro backed from the room, slowly followed by Gonzales and his soldiers. Suddenly, Zorro pushed the captain from him and darted into the darkness. Bullets whistled past his head, but above the wind that blew from the far-off sea came the sound of his laughter.

Zorro galloped away from the town. He rode for five miles and the soldiers did not gain on him at all. But there were no trails from the highway and he wanted to double back toward Reina de Los Angeles. Beyond a bend, Zorro stopped and turned his horse around. Then he dug in his spurs. The horse sprang forward like lightning and ran straight at two of the soldiers, knocking them from their horses. In this way, Zorro rode back down the highway, knocking each soldier from his horse as he passed.

"An excellent trick!" he said to his horse.

CHAPTER SEVEN

A Public Punishment

On the crest of a small hill on the highway stood a hacienda that now belonged to the mission of San Gabriel. Franciscan monks lived there, under the guidance of a friar called Felipe. The ranch made a good profit by keeping cattle and selling their hides.

Gonzales knew that the friars were friendly toward Senor Zorro because he helped the poor. He decided to stop at the hacienda and check for signs of him. He scattered his men around the land and barns. Then he rode up the steps to the veranda and knocked on the door with his sword.

Fray Felipe, a tall man of over sixty, opened it, shading a candle from the wind. "Why do you ride your horse on my veranda?" he asked.

"We are chasing Senor Zorro," Gonzales replied. "Have you heard a horseman gallop past here recently?"

"I have not," Fray Felipe said coldly. "But I know of him because he helps the poor."

"I do not like the tone of your voice," Gonzales said. "I shall order my men to search your house."

As Gonzales pushed through the door with his soldiers, a man rose from the couch in the corner of the room and stepped into the candlelight.

It was Don Diego.

"I have come to visit my friend for peace and quiet," he sighed. "These are difficult times. Is there no place in this country where I can listen to music and poetry?"

"Corn mush and goat's milk!" Gonzales cried. "Don Diego, you are my good friend and a true caballero, have you seen this Senor Zorro?"

"I have not, my sergeant," Don Diego replied. "And now I suppose you will continue chasing around the countryside making a noise?"

"We shall take up the chase again," Gonzales said angrily. "I seek revenge now, not just a reward."

The next morning, the sun was shining brightly in the town and blossom scented the air. Don Diego, who had returned home, was saying goodbye to his guests.

"I am sorry that your daughter does not wish to marry me," he told Don Carlos.

"Do not give up hope," he replied. "A woman changes her mind as often as she changes her hair."

As they drove away, Don Diego glanced up the trail that ran toward the road to San Gabriel. He saw two men on horseback – and a man walking between them, tied to the horses.

It was Fray Felipe.

He had been forced to walk all the way from his hacienda and his clothes were ragged and dusty. People crowded around to make fun of him as he was taken to the magistrate's office.

Don Diego pushed his way through the crowd. "What is happening?" he cried. "This man is Fray Felipe, a godly man, and my good friend."

"He is a cheat," one of the soldiers said.

A short trial began. An evil-looking man, a hide dealer, complained that he had bought ten hides from Fray Felipe, but found that they had not been dried properly. When he had asked for his money back, Fray Felipe had refused.

"The hides were good," Fray Felipe protested. "I promised to return his money when he returned the hides. But I have no more to say. You have already decided that I am guilty."

"Silence!" the magistrate said. "I sentence you to fifteen lashes in the plaza."

Don Diego's face turned pale as the friar was dragged to the whipping post in the plaza. There his robe was torn from his back. As his friend was whipped, Don Diego mopped the sweat from his brow. "These are difficult times," he said to himself. "There is no peace anywhere. I shall visit my father's hacienda today. Nobody will bother me there."

That same evening, the hide dealer and his assistant began their journey back home. As they neared the crest of the hill behind the town, they met a man on a horse blocking their way.

"'Tis Senor Zorro!" the dealer cried, his eyes bulging with fear. "By the saints, senor, do not bother me! I am only a poor man! Just yesterday, I lost my money to a dishonest friar."

"Silence!" Zorro shouted. "I do not want your money. I know all about that trial today. You are a liar and a thief. Step forward."

The dealer moved closer. Suddenly he began to beg for mercy as Zorro took a whip from under his cloak. "Turn your back to me!" Zorro ordered, raising his whip. He whipped them both soundly. "Let us hope that you have learned your lesson!" he said. "Now be on your way."

Zorro looked at the town from the crest of the hill. The candles had already been lit in the tavern. He rode until he reached the plaza. Then he rode right up to the tavern door.

"Landlord!" he shouted. "If the magistrate is in there, tell him a caballero outside wishes to speak to him."

Soon the magistrate staggered outside – and looked up into two glittering eyes behind a black mask.

"Not a sound," Zorro said, holding up his pistol, "or you die. I have come to punish you. You passed judgment on an innocent man today. Now you shall have the same punishment."

"How dare…" the magistrate began.

"Silence!" Zorro ordered.

Zorro forced five men to tie the magistrate to the whipping post and whip him fifteen times. After the groaning magistrate had been carried home, Zorro rode back to the tavern and ordered the landlord to bring some wine.

"Do not tell anybody what has happened," he said.

But the landlord told all the men in the tavern. They drew out their swords and rushed outside. Zorro, sitting on his horse, saw the light flash from their blades. He dug his spurs into his horse and it reared, scattering the men. With one hand he drew out his sword and fought them hard. With the other, he picked up the whip and lashed the landlord for betraying him.

Then he started to back across the plaza, taking off his sombrero. "There are not enough of you to make this fight interesting," he shouted, laughing. With a mocking bow, he turned his horse and rode away.

The town of Reina de Los Angeles was in uproar. The shrieks of the landlord had woken everybody up. Now many young gentlemen crowded into the tavern to hear what had happened. Captain Ramon rushed down from the army barracks.

"My men are never here when Senor Zorro appears," he complained. "I have sent a rider to bring back Sergeant Gonzales."

"We can help you!" the young men told him. "We want to form a posse to hunt down Senor Zorro."

CHAPTER EIGHT

The Young Avengers

It was long after nightfall when Don Diego arrived at his father's hacienda. Don Alejandro was dining alone and he was pleased to see his son. But he was not pleased to hear that the Senorita Lolita had refused to marry him.

"Is the Vega blood to die out because you will have no children?" he asked angrily. "Court her properly, son. Be a man or I shall leave all my money to the friars." He paused. "Sometimes I wish you had the courage and spirit of this Senor Zorro. He has principles and he fights for them. Why are you such a dreamer?"

"I have been a dutiful son, father," Don Diego replied. "Can we talk of something else? My nerves are on edge."

"I wish you had been wilder," his father said. "When I was your age, nobody laughed at me. You must be more of a man, Diego. By the saints, what is that?"

They heard the sound of horses outside. A servant opened the door and ten young gentlemen came in, carrying pistols and swords.

"Good evening, Don Alejandro!" they said. "We are looking for Senor Zorro, the highwayman! Has he been here? Did you pass him on the way, Diego?"

"By the saints, I came here for some peace and quiet!" Don Diego replied. "No, I did not see him."

The servants brought out jugs of wine and the young men put down their weapons and began to talk. They forgot about capturing Zorro. At last Don Diego stood up.

"I am tired after my journey," he said, "so I shall go to bed."

Don Diego's father frowned and twisted his moustache. "Why cannot my son be like other young men?" he asked himself.

The young men were singing and laughing loudly as they drank. "If only Senor Zorro was with us now!" they shouted.

"He is here!" a voice said. It came from a cloaked and masked figure at the veranda door. He was pointing a pistol at them.

Silence fell in the room.

"You drink and enjoy yourselves while there is wrongdoing all around you," Zorro sneered. "Live up to your noble names. Take your swords and fight the wrong in our country. Stop the thieving politicians. Look after the friars. Be men! Be real caballeros and protect the weak."

Some of the men jumped to their feet. "By the saints, it would be fun!" they shouted.

"No, it would be treason," another said.

"It is not treason to rid the country of evil men," Zorro said. "I will lead you."

"Are you a gentleman?" they asked. "Where is your family?"

"That must remain a secret for now," Zorro replied.

"Wait!" another cried. "We are guests here. We cannot talk of such things unless Don Alejandro agrees."

"I give you my support," Don Alejandro said.

Cheers filled the room. "We shall call ourselves the Avengers!" the caballeros shouted. "We shall drive out our thieving politicians! Tell us what to do, Senor Zorro."

"Do not talk of this to anybody," he replied. "Return to Reina de Los Angeles in the morning and say that you could not catch me. But be ready. I shall send word to you at the right time."

"Agreed!" they shouted together.

Senor Zorro bowed to them. "Adios, caballeros!" he said. He darted through the veranda door and slammed it behind him. Then the young men sat down to talk of all the wrongs they would put right. They had often thought of these things before, but they had never joined together to take action.

"Senor Zorro has come to us at the right time," they said.

Don Alejandro listened. "My son is asleep," he thought bitterly. "He should have been part of this."

At that moment, Don Diego came slowly into the room, yawning and rubbing his eyes. "Can a man not sleep in peace?" he complained.

"Sit down, Diego!" his father said. "I want to tell you what has just happened. At last you will have a chance to show what sort of blood flows in your veins."

CHAPTER NINE

To the Rescue!

The Governor of California set out for Reina de Los Angeles as soon as he received Captain Ramon's letter. Captain Ramon saluted him at the entrance to the barracks and told him what had been happening during the last few days.

"Don Carlos Pulido and some of the friars are protecting Senor Zorro, I know it," he explained. "They must be telling him where my soldiers are, for he only appears when they are somewhere else."

"Then send soldiers to arrest Don Carlos," the Governor said, "and his wife and daughter. It will teach everybody a lesson."

The Pulido family entered the town under arrest. Their hearts were bursting with grief, but they did not show it. They held their heads high, looked straight ahead and ignored the jeers of the soldiers. But when they reached the prison, the Governor had another lesson to teach them. He had paid local people to insult the Pulidos by throwing mud at them.

An hour later, Don Diego also made his way to the army barracks to pay his respects to the Governor. He was dressed in the latest fashion and in his right hand he carried a lace handkerchief. He greeted the Governor politely. Then he added, "I think you may have insulted me when you imprisoned the Pulido family. I am almost engaged to Senorita Lolita."

"Come and look for a wife in the north, caballero," the Governor replied. "Our women are far more beautiful." He leaned forward. "Perhaps you will change your mind when I tell you that Don Carlos has been shielding Senor Zorro."

"That is astonishing!" Don Diego replied.

"While you were visiting your father, Senor Zorro was in your house, speaking to the senorita Lolita and wounding Captain Ramon."

"By the saints, I cannot believe it!" Don Diego exclaimed.

"I shall keep the Pulidos in prison until Zorro is caught. I shall force him to confess and they will all stand trial. I hope you see the sense of this."

"I do," Don Diego replied. "These are difficult times. All the enemies of our country should be punished."

Don Diego said farewell. Crossing the plaza, he met the young men who had been drinking at his father's hacienda.

"Ha! Don Diego!" they called. "Has the man who is to be our leader sent you a message today? We expect him to sort out this Pulido business."

"No, and I hope he does not send one," Don Diego replied. "My head aches and I do not feel well. I fear a fever. I do not want any adventure tonight."

One hour after dusk, a servant repeated this message to one of the caballeros:

There is a fox in the area and a gentleman wishes to talk about it. He will be waiting on the San Gabriel road.

The young man hurried there at once. He found Senor Zorro sitting on his horse, wrapped in his cloak, his face masked.

"The time has come, senor," Zorro said. "Tell your friends that all men who are loyal to me must meet at midnight in the little valley beyond the hill."

Just before midnight, the caballeros began slipping from the town one at a time, each riding his best horse, each armed with a sword and pistol – and each wearing a mask. Only Don Diego could not be there. He was in bed with a fever.

"We must rescue the Pulido family," Zorro said. "There is no moon tonight. So we shall be safe if we enter the town quietly. We shall each have our own task – mine is to rescue the Senorita Lolita. Then we will scatter into hiding." But when they reached the prison, Don Carlos refused to leave.

"I shall not run away, senor," he said. "I am already accused of helping you. How will it look if I leave with you now?"

"This is no time for argument," Zorro replied. "I am not alone. There are gentlemen with me who feel it is wrong for you to be here." He turned round and shouted, "Caballeros!" Four men hurried in and carried out Don Carlos and his wife.

Senor Zorro bowed to Senorita Lolita. "Trust me," he said.

"To love is to trust, senor," she replied.

By the time the three rescued prisoners were on horseback, the guard had called for help. Sergeant Gonzales and his men rushed from the tavern firing their pistols, but nobody was hit. Zorro rode away as fast as his horse could go with Senorita Lolita in the saddle in front of him.

"I knew you would rescue me, senor," she whispered.

Zorro spurred his horse ahead of all the others, leading the way to the highway. Here, he and the caballeros scattered and rode on through the darkness.

As Zorro reached the crest of the hill above the town, he looked down. The army barracks blazed with light and a trumpet sounded to call the soldiers. He heard the sound of galloping horses and knew that every soldier would be after him. He turned his horse, pressed his spurs and rode on furiously through the night. The moon began to rise and Zorro knew that he could be seen against the brightening sky. He spurred on his horse harder – until he could see Fray Felipe's hacienda glistening in the moonlight.

"I am putting my trust in this man," he thought. "I hope he will not let me down."

CHAPTER TEN

Zorro Unmasked

Senor Zorro banged loudly on Fray Felipe's door with his fist. At last, the friar opened it and stepped back in astonishment at the sight of the masked man and a girl.

"I am Senor Zorro," he said. "I hope you can help me – and the Senorita Lolita. She is the daughter of Don Carlos Pulido. He is a friend of the friars. The Governor ordered him and his family to be thrown into prison today."

"I can," Fray Felipe replied. "I owe you a great debt for punishing those who treated me badly. And may the saints bless you for what you have done today."

As Zorro ran to his horse, he saw soldiers galloping down the driveway. They surrounded him, their swords flashing.

"Take him alive if you can!" Gonzales shouted.

As he fought with his sword, Zorro fell from his horse. He managed to fight his way back to the shadows of the trees. Then he dashed from one tree to another, then jumped onto one of the soldier's horses. Zorro rode toward the barn.

"I have just enough time to play a trick," he thought.

In the shadow of the barn, he jumped from the horse and made the animal carry on running. The soldiers rode after it. Then Zorro ran up the hill giving a loud piercing cry and his own horse galloped toward him. Zorro spurred his horse on across the fields. The soldiers were now charging him on both sides. But he gained the lead and soon reached the highway leading back to Reina de Los Angeles. The moon went in and he rode even harder.

Gonzales knew that he could not overtake Zorro now. "I shall gain some favor with the Governor by returning to Fray Felipe and recapturing Senorita Lolita," he told himself.

The soldiers searched the friar's house from top to bottom, but they found no one. Then Gonzales noticed a pile of hides in the corner of the room which seemed to be moving. As the soldiers went to search, Senorita Lolita stood up and faced them, holding up a knife.

"I shall never go back to that foul prison," she cried, "not now or at any other time. I would rather plunge this knife into my heart. The Governor will get only my dead body. Now stand back against the wall."

Gonzales and his men had no choice. They moved back. Senorita Lolita darted through the door.

"After her!" Gonzales cried. He hurled himself across the room. But Fray Felipe had been quiet for too long. He tripped up the sergeant and his men crashed into him. By the time they had reached the door, Senorita Lolita was riding away as fast as the wind.

Zorro had another little adventure planned for that night. He rode for two hours until he reached the crest of the hill above Reina de Los Angeles. He circled the town slowly and approached the army barracks from behind. Captain Ramon was in his office, waiting for his men to return.

Just as before, he turned round when he heard the door open – and saw the eyes of Zorro glittering through his mask. Zorro dragged him onto his horse and rode to the house where the Governor was staying. There he forced Ramon to admit to the lies that he had told in his letter. He was pale with rage, knowing that his career was now over.

"And you have insulted an innocent girl," Zorro added. "For that, you will fight me."

Captain Ramon drew out his sword and threw himself upon Zorro. But Zorro stood his ground and fought back. He was eager for the duel to be over because it was almost dawn.

"Kill him, Ramon," the Governor shouted, "and I will give you back your job."

"Insulter of girls!" Zorro taunted. "Coward! Liar! Ha! Fight, dog!"

The ringing steel of this life-and-death struggle were the only sounds in the room. Ramon lunged at Zorro, thrusting his sword toward him. But he missed by the fraction of an inch. Like the tongue of a snake, Zorro thrust his blade at the captain's forehead. Three times he thrust his sword, until a letter of blood appeared.

"The Mark of Zorro!" he cried. "You will wear it forever, captain."

And with a final thrust, he ran his sword through Captain Ramon's heart.

"He will never insult a senorita again," Zorro said.

Dawn had come and the sky was clear. It was a bad time to escape. As Zorro prepared to leave, he looked around him. Soldiers were riding toward the town down every trail.

"I have stayed too long," he thought. "Now I am trapped."

Suddenly, Gonzales saw him and raised the alarm. Zorro spurred his horse and dashed across the plaza, making for the highway. Gonzales and his troops rushed to cut him off. Zorro turned back to the plaza and made for a hill behind the town and more soldiers galloped to meet him. Zigzagging as he rode, Zorro managed to reach the highway. But here was a new threat. Straight toward him came a rider followed closely by more soldiers.

Zorro was forced to turn back. Gonzales was riding straight at him. As he gripped his sword and prepared to fight, Zorro glanced quickly at the rider behind him. It was Senorita Lolita.

"Stay close behind me!" he shouted. "We shall have to ride straight at Gonzales. We have no choice."

They rode fast through the soldiers, forcing them to fall over one another, and reached the plaza. Now every trail out of town was guarded by soldiers, blocking their escape.

"To the tavern!" Zorro cried.

As they galloped across the plaza, Senorita Lolita's horse

staggered. Zorro caught her in his arms and pushed open the door. He bolted all the doors and windows.

"It may be the end," Zorro said. "I do not care about myself, but you, Senorita…I…"

"I would rather die with you," she replied.

Zorro glanced through the window. The soldiers were surrounding the tavern now. The Governor was striding across the plaza shouting out his orders. And down the San Gabriel trail came Don Alejandro Vega to pay his respects to the visitor.

"Even my father will be at my death," Zorro whispered. "Where are my brave caballeros now?"

"Will they help you?" Senorita Lolita asked.

"I do not think so," he said. "They thought this was just an adventure. I doubt they will tell the Governor what they really think. No, I fight alone."

"Not alone, senor," she replied. "I am by your side."

"Forget me, senorita," he said. "Agree to marry Don Diego Vega. Then the Governor will let you go. You will have all you need."

"Everything except love," she said.

The attack on the tavern door began. Zorro ran his sword through a crack in the door – and emptied his pistol – but the soldiers continued to shoot back.

"It is almost the end, senor," Senorita Lolita whispered. "Let me see your face.

Zorro sighed and started to lift the bottom of his mask.

But suddenly, the battering and shooting stopped and shouts came from the plaza. Zorro looked through the window again. More than twenty men, wearing cloaks and masks and feathered hats, were galloping toward the tavern. And each man carried a sword studded with jewels.

"Wait!" they cried. "There is a better way than this."

"Ha!" the Governor shouted. "So all the noble men of the south have come to show their loyalty to a highwayman!"

"We have talked among ourselves," the young men replied, "and we have decided it is wrong to treat the friars badly. It is wrong to take land from our people. That is why we rode with Senor Zorro. What do you say, your Excellency?"

"Wait until we have captured this Senor Zorro," the Governor replied.

"He has done nothing wrong," the caballeros cried together. "We demand a complete pardon for him."

"Never!" the Governor shouted. He turned and saw Don Diego's father. "Don Alejandro, you are the most influential man in the south. Tell these young men to go home."

"I agree with them!" he replied in a voice of thunder.

"Then I must pardon Senor Zorro," the Governor said weakly.

The caballeros roared with delight and got down from their horses. "Did you hear, Senor Zorro?" they called. "Open the door. You are now a free man."

Slowly the battered door opened and Zorro stepped out

with Senorita Lolita on his arm. He took off his sombrero and bowed low.

"By the saints, he is a gentleman!" Gonzales cried.

"Show your face!" the Governor ordered.

Zorro put up his hand and ripped off his mask. The caballeros gasped in delight. The soldiers swore. And Don Alejandro Vega was full of pride.

"Don Diego!" he gasped. "My son!"

Don Diego sighed and spoke in a tired voice, "These are difficult times. Can a man not have any peace?" He glanced down at Senorita Lolita. "There will be no need for Senor Zorro to ride any more. A married man should take care of his life."

And he stooped to kiss her in front of them all.

"Corn mush and goat's milk!" Sergeant Gonzales cried.

Key Characters

Pedro Gonzales (PAY-droh gon-ZAH-lez) A sergeant.

Don Diego Vega (don dee-AY-goh VAY-geh) A nobleman.

Senor Zorro (sen-YOR ZO-roh) A masked stranger.

Don Carlos Pulido (don KAR-los pul-EE-doh) A friend of
Don Diego Vega.

Lolita (loh-LEE-teh) Daughter of Don Carlos Pulido.

Ramon (ram-ON) An army captain.

Don Alejandro (don aleh-HAND-roh) Father of Don
Diego Vega.

The Governor of California

Key Locations

Reina de Los Angeles A town in southern California.

Key Terms

(with pronunciation guide)

avenging (av-ENJ-ing) Taking revenge. pp25, 36

barracks (BAR-aks) Buildings where soldiers are housed. pp19, 25, 33, 38, 44

crest The top of a hill. pp28, 41, 43

duel (DOO-el) A fight between two people. pp26, 44

fate Destiny. p6

friars (FRY-erz) Monks. pp28, 29, 34, 35, 42, 47

hides The skins of animals such as cows and goats. pp28, 30, 31, 43

highwayman (HY-way-man) Someone who holds up vehicles on the road and robs the passengers. pp11, 19, 21, 47

inherit (in-HEH-rit) To receive something, such as money or property, after the previous owner's death. p9

landlord (LAND-lord) A person who runs a bar. pp6, 7, 32

lunging (LUNJ-ing) Lurching forward. p10

magistrate (MAJ-is-trayt) A local judge. pp30, 32

missions (MISH-uns) Groups of people aiming to spread Christianity within an area. pp9, 11, 28

posse (POSS-ee) Group. p33

ranch An area of land where cows or sheep are kept. p33

siesta (see-ES-ta) A short sleep during the day. p16

spur To use spiked wheels on the heels of a boot to urge a horse forward. pp27, 41, 43, 45

tavern (TA-vern) An inn. pp6, 7, 15, 32, 45, 46

treason (TREE-sun) Traitorous behavior toward a country or ruler. 35

veranda (veh-RAN-deh) An open area with a roof on the outside of a building. pp29, 35, 37

Spanish Words

(Spanish words used in the story)

adios	goodbye
caballero	gentleman
Don	Mr.
fray	friar, monk
hacienda	cattle ranch
plaza	a village or town square
senor/senores	Mr./gentleman
senorita	Miss/madam
sombrero	hat with a large round brim
zorro	ox

For More Information

http://www.vintagelibrary.com/pulpfiction/authors/Johnston-McCulley.php

A web site with links to information about the life and career of Johnston McCulley and the character of Zorro that he created.

http://history.sandiego.edu/gen/filmnotes/markofzorro.html

Information about the movie *The Mark of Zorro*. The movie was based on the original story about Zorro, written by Johnston McCulley and published in a weeky magazine.

For Further Reading

The Mark of Zorro by Johnston McCulley (Penguin Classics, 2005)

The Man Who Changed Rooms by Johnston McCulley (Wildside Press, 2008)

Index

About the Reteller

Pauline Francis was a teacher of French, and then a school librarian before she became an author of books for children and young people. As well as her retellings of classic novels, in the Foundation Classics series, her books include stories for children learning English as a foreign language, stories for younger readers, and historical novels for older readers.

You can find more great fiction and nonfiction from Windmill Books at windmillbks.com